The Winter King
and the
Summer Queen

written by Mary Lister

illustrated by Diana Mayo

Barefoot Books
Celebrating Art and Story

In the beginning, long long ago, the sky was split into two kingdoms. One kingdom was warm and sunny. The other one was cold and dark.

Land of the Flaming Sun

The warm kingdom was called the Land of the Flaming Sun, and the cold kingdom was called the Land of Icy Darkness.

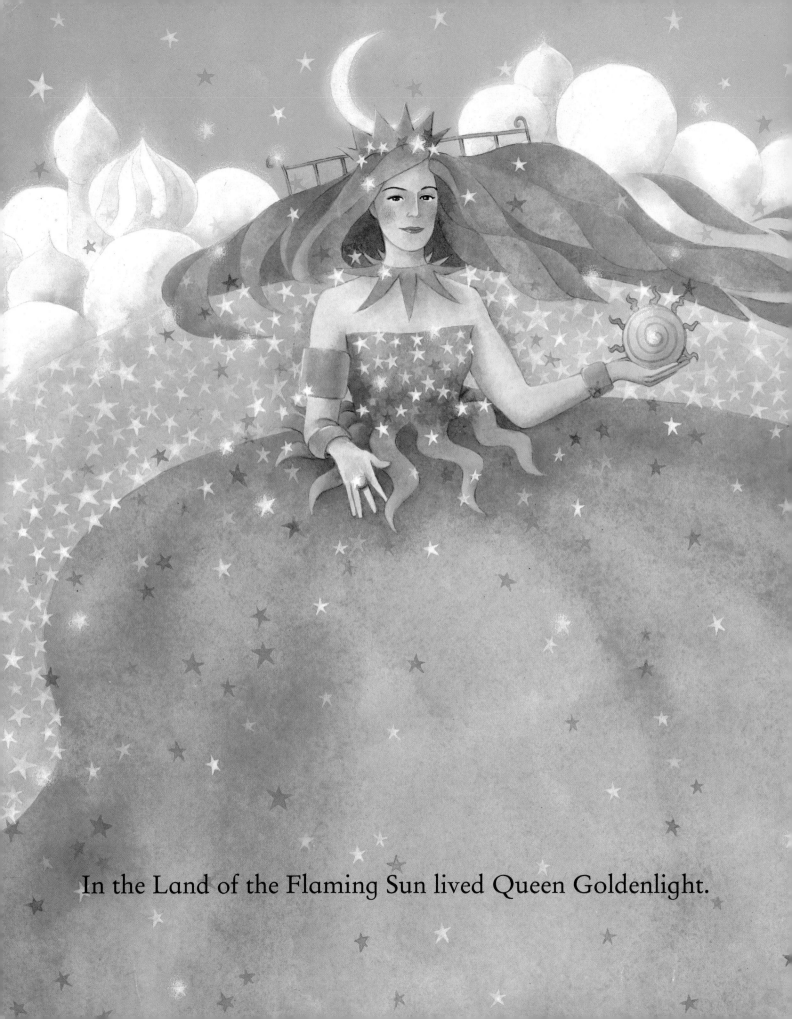

In the Land of the Flaming Sun lived Queen Goldenlight.

Her eyes were like blazing stars.

She wore the moon in her crown.

Her smile was like a sunbeam.

Her hair was like flaming fire,

and her cloak was made of
galaxies of a million, tiny,
glimmering, shimmering stars.

Her palace was made of bright
white light.

Queen Goldenlight had lots of friends.

Serena Sky

Mrs Springtime

Callum Cloud

Steven Star

Master Moonbeam

Sunshine Sally

Far away across the sky, King Icicle ruled in the Land of Icy Darkness. No one messed around with King Icicle.

He was a fierce frost giant.

His heart was made of snow and frost.

His eyes were like ice splinters.

On his feet were spiky icicle boots.

He wore trousers made of glaciers and a huge, snow-blown cloak.

King Icicle's companions were quite different
to Queen Goldenlight's. They were:

Mr Thunderbolt

Miss Twister

Harry Hurricane

Danny Drizzle

Akshya Monsoon

Philippa Freezo

Queen Goldenlight and her friends liked to warm the Earth, sending light and heat to all the men, women and children. They played games and sang songs all the time. While they played, the birds sang, the bees buzzed and the butterflies danced.

But King Icicle and his companions were gloomy and cold. No one said 'hello', they just said 'Brrrhhh!' They didn't sing songs or play games. They just played ice music, but that made the land even colder.

King Icicle's favourite sport was to send storms down to the Earth.

Thunder boomed – crash, crash!

Snow fell – shiver, shiver!

The people on Earth got so cold that they all turned into snow men and snow women and snow babies. The birds stopped singing, the animals shivered and the fish froze in the ponds and rivers. Everyone was very unhappy.

When Queen Goldenlight looked down at the Earth and saw how cold everyone was, she said, 'We must do something!'

To help the fish, she sent a magic fish.

To help the birds,
she sent a magic bird.

To help the animals,
she sent a magic hare.

And she gave each of them a ray of endless sunshine to
help them in their task.

The bird flew around the Earth, the hare bounded across the frozen land, and the fish swam bravely through the icy rivers.

And in and out of the water, air and earth they wove rays of endless sunshine, making a beautiful stripy rainbow.

When King Icicle saw the rainbow he
was furious. He sent storms to blow it down.

Winds blew – phew, phew!
Lightning crackled – flash, flash!
Thunder boomed – crash, crash!
Snow fell – shiver, shiver!

But nothing happened.

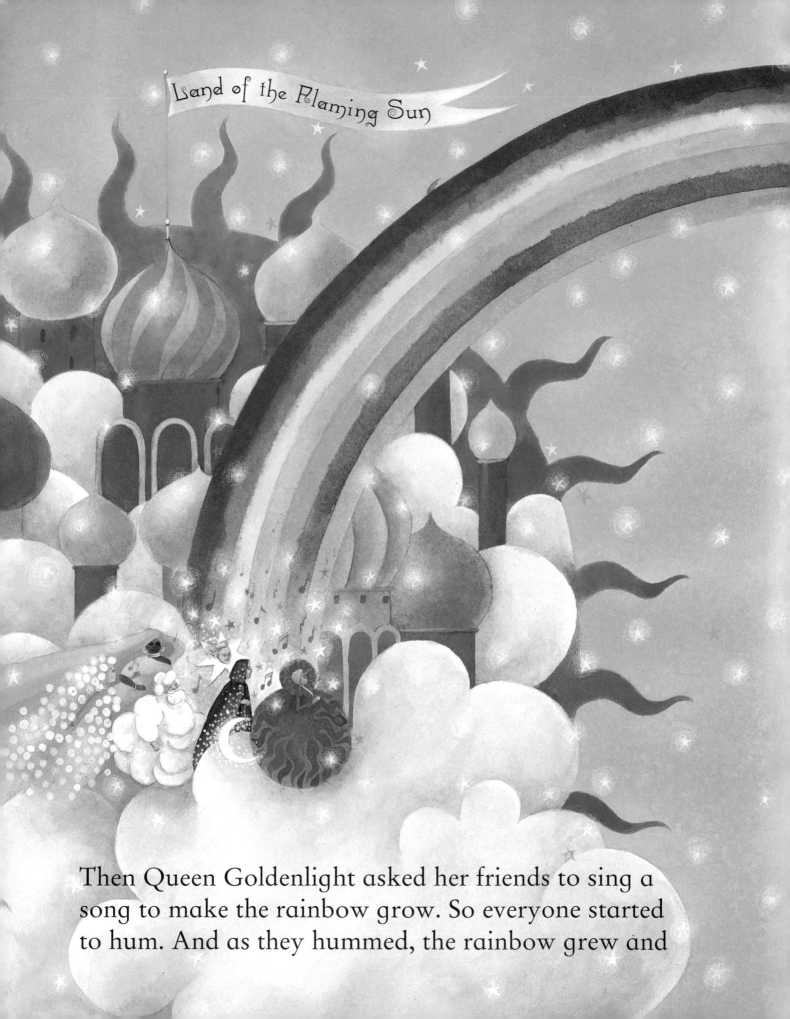

Land of the Flaming Sun

Then Queen Goldenlight asked her friends to sing a song to make the rainbow grow. So everyone started to hum. And as they hummed, the rainbow grew and

Land of Icy Darkness

grew until it became a huge bridge between the Land of the Flaming Sun and the Land of Icy Darkness, right over the Earth. It was beautiful!

When the people in the Land of the Sun
and the people in the Land of Ice saw the
rainbow, they all wanted to run up it. Even
King Icicle's heart started to melt when he
saw the rainbow. He wanted to climb it!
So up he ran in his pointy icicle boots.

As he ran, the boots started to melt, squelch, squelch, squelch! And King Icicle actually laughed! At first it came out as an icy cackle, then it crackled and cracked and began to melt, until it had become a really jolly, happy chuckle. Ha ha ha! Ho ho ho!

At the top of the rainbow, King Icicle met Queen Goldenlight. 'May I have the honour of a dance?' he asked, bowing low.

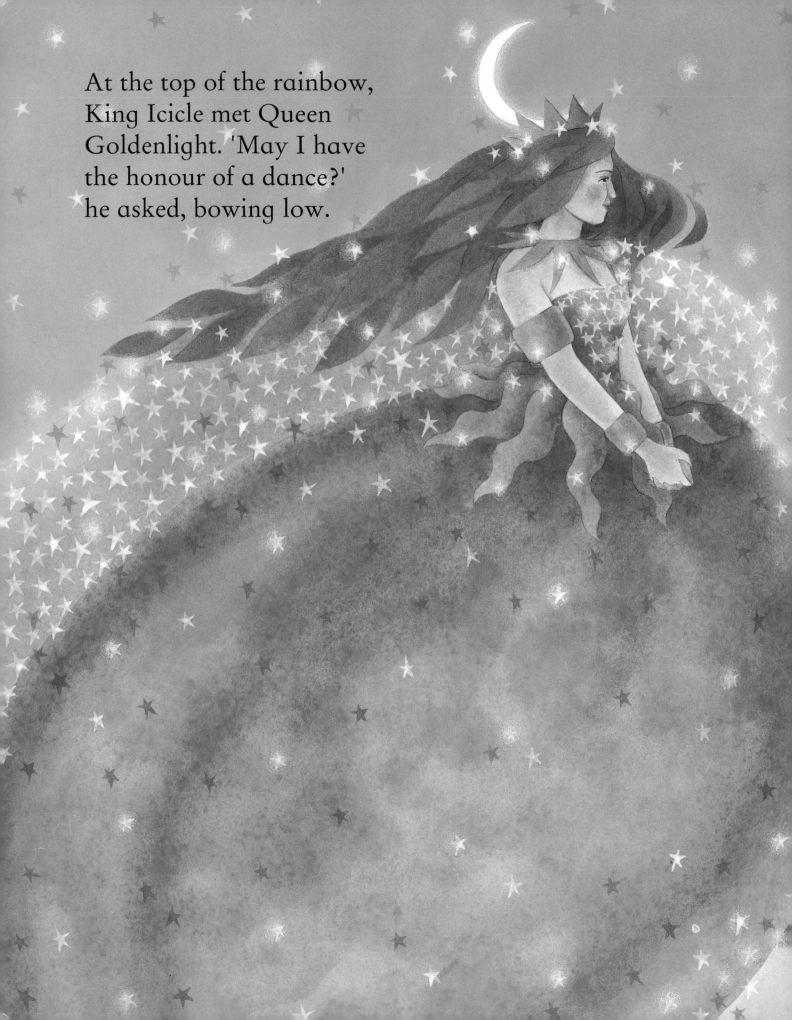

'I shall dance with you if you can answer this riddle',
the Queen replied.
'Red, orange, yellow; blue, indigo, violet, green,
The King can dance over it, and so can the Queen!
Storms cannot destroy it, although their power is great.
Answer me this riddle before I count to eight!'

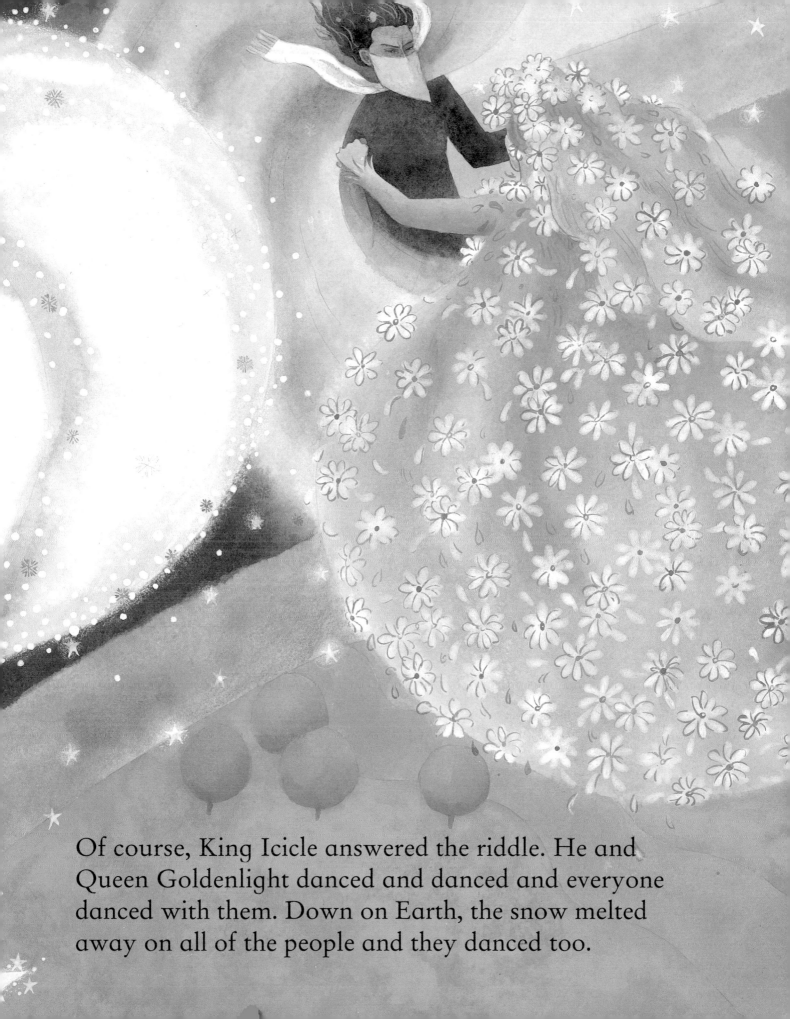

Of course, King Icicle answered the riddle. He and
Queen Goldenlight danced and danced and everyone
danced with them. Down on Earth, the snow melted
away on all of the people and they danced too.

Afterwards, the King and the Queen came to an agreement. From then on, all of the weather could share the Earth. The King became winter, and he was to look after the Earth for six months of the year. The Queen became summer, and she was to look after it for the other six months. They were to share everything, so that we have a mixture of cold and warmth, sunshine and rain, light and darkness. And now, we do! But sometimes, just very occasionally, King Icicle forgets himself and sends out too many of his cold spirits. And that's why we get storms and hurricanes.

Publisher's Note

This story was originally written for a literacy project for 4 – 7 year-olds at the West Yorkshire Playhouse and was designed to extend children's vocabulary, use of language and sense of story structure and characterisation. There are numerous ways in which the text can be used to explore and enhance children's understanding of the story, both in the classroom and at home. Please visit the Barefoot Books website, *www.*barefootbooks.*com*, for an array of teaching ideas and crafts suggestions — from weaving a rainbow mural to writing a wind song, there is a rich offering of activities online for children to enjoy and learn from.

To my mother and father, who are my favourite parents — M. L.
To Jake, for all your love and support — D. M.

Barefoot Books
124 Walcot Street
Bath BA1 5BG

Text copyright © 2002 by Mary Lister
Illustrations copyright © 2002 by Diana Mayo
The moral right of Mary Lister to be identified as the author and
Diana Mayo to be identified as the illustrator of this work has been asserted

This book was typeset in Garamond Infant 19 on 24 point
The illustrations were prepared in acrylics on hotpress watercolour paper

Graphic design by Judy Linard, London
Colour separation by Grafiscan, Verona
Printed and bound in Singapore by Tien Wah Press (Pte) Ltd

This book has been printed on 100% acid-free paper

ISBN 1 84148 358 3

British Cataloguing-in-Publication Data: a catalogue record for this book
is available from the British Library

3 5 7 9 8 6 4 2